Moonstones and Whalebones

C. S. NOLAN

Copyright @2021 by Cynthia Nolan

All rights reserved. No part of this book may be reproduced in any form or by any electronic or mechanical means, including information storage and retrieval systems, without permission in writing from the publisher, except by reviewers, who may quote brief passages in a review.

This publication contains the opinions and ideas of its author. It is intended to provide helpful and informative material on the subjects addressed in the publication. The author and publisher specifically disclaim all responsibility for any liability, loss or risk, personal or otherwise, which is incurred as a consequence, directly or indirectly, of the use and application of any of the contents of this book.

WORKBOOK PRESS LLC
187 E Warm Springs Rd,
Suite B285, Las Vegas, NV 89119, USA

Website: https://workbookpress.com/
Hotline: 1-888-818-4856
Email: admin@workbookpress.com

Ordering Information:
Quantity sales. Special discounts are available on quantity purchases by corporations, associations, and others. For details, contact the publisher at the address above.

ISBN-13:   978-1-954753-63-1 (Paperback Version)
              978-1-954753-64-8 (Digital Version)

REV. DATE: 24.02.2021

Table Of Contents

Chapter 1 Moonstones ························· 07

Chapter 2 Old Man Drake ······················ 10

Chapter 3 Marine Research ···················· 14

Chapter 4 Family Problems ···················· 18

Chapter 5 Daniel's Escape ····················· 19

Chapter 6 A Mother's Love ···················· 21

Chapter 7 Good Food, Happy Home ············ 23

Chapter 8 Fearless Crew ······················· 27

Chapter 9 The Tempest ························ 28

Chapter 10 Mainlanders Enduring the Wait ······ 30

Chapter 11 Completing the Legend ·············· 32

Chapter 12 Daniel and Vincent Become Heroes ··· 38

Chapter 13 A Father's Love ···················· 43

Chapter 14 Honoring Our Heroes ··············· 44

About the Author ····························· 46

CHAPTER 1

Moonstones

The warm rays were illuminated through the cool mist that floated gently over the rolling California coastline. The light flickered over the dark blue water as it moved back and forth over the pebble-covered shore. The smooth sand polished each unique, glistening pebble. These pebbles, stones carried over time from distant shores, were of a special and treasured gemstone called moonstones, emerald in nature but slightly iridescent, reflecting colors of the spectrum. Some were green, others were white, and even a few had tones of opal and pearl. These were the stones of Moonstone Beach, quite spectacular and only occurring in a few places on Earth: Brazil, India, Mexico, Myanmar, Sri Lanka, and the European Alps. Of course in North America, it was the Florida state gem and also appeared in California. It was quite noted for its charm and ruggedness.

The moonstones has a historical connection with travel. It was once known as the "Traveler's Stone," used to guard against the perils of travel. The Romans admired them and believed they were solidified rays of the moon. They are of a feldspar variety, uneven to conchoidal. On Mohs scale of mineral hardness, they are 6.0. Their luster is opalescent with streaks of white. They have a specific gravity of 2.61. The scientific name, Potassium Aluminum Silicate. Moonstones are crystals that vary in color—appearing in gray, white, green, and pink.

* * *

Daniel called out, "Mom, I've found one."

Every hour on the hour for the past twelve hours, Daniel's mom, Erica, had been taking recordings of ocean temperatures,. It was a painstaking task. She was feeling fatigue, but with the heart of a warrior, she completed the job and returned a reply to her son.

"Daniel, which variety is it?"

Daniel was absorbed in the quest of finding the different types of moonstone, all unique and varying in several ways. "Look, Mom, this one shimmers like an opal. And look at this green one. See the veins and the marvelous shape?"

Erica looked at her tall and lanky son; he was almost fourteen years old with sandy blond, uncombed hair that complemented his handsome, boyish face. He was the spitting image of her brother, Matthew, and he was not a thing like his dad, Vincent, except for that sparkle in his blue eyes. But Daniel had the mind of a scientist and the heart of an artist, very much like his father before he became a mysterious workaholic.

Erica bent down to examine the stones. With perceptive eyes and delicate hands, she examined the stones. "Brilliant and how unique. Where did you find these exactly?"

"Here, Mom, next to this boulder covered with the green moss. There are many, and most have that opal glow."

"Nice, Daniel, but unusual—these two especially. Most are dark green, and here we have the white one. Most magnificent. Did you record your data?"

"Yes, Mother," Daniel replied with some exaggeration. "And, yes, I did record the time, date, and placement with illustrations. Don't forget, Mom. I'm almost fourteen."

"Daniel, all right. Just checking, love. I really do not think I need permission to act like a concerned mother or even a mentor."

As Erica moved slowly to her work area, deep in thought, she realized her son reminded her that he would follow her footsteps. *He really shares very few traits with his father,* she thought.

Vincent had changed over the years. Though at first he'd been attentive and devoted, he became distant after Daniel was born. He worked extremely long hours and seemed to be away most of the time. As always, Erica took charge and accepted the change. Even over the next ten years, Vincent continued to be distant and self-absorbed. Erica was not bothered, but she still saw the need of fatherly devotion in her young son.

His father, she thought, *is the only man I could love and resent at the same time.*

CHAPTER 2

Old Man Drake

Daniel was a happy kid—busy, curious, quiet, and cautious. But he was not timid. He was popular on the island, not just with his peers but with the island people as well, especially Old Man Drake Clark. Some said the old man was a little touched in the head, but both Erica and Daniel knew better.

The old man was a storyteller, and boy howdy, could he tell a story. Erica and Daniel frequented his garden often, seeking the solace of a kind heart and enjoying the affections of an older generation. Daniel also spent time helping the old man, fetching his mail, pulling weeds, and doing other errands. Daniel needed his father, and the old man was a grandfather image who took the dual role of father and grandfather.

The old man also fascinated Daniel with his stories, especially about the island. There was a legend shared among the old island people and the new island folk who enjoyed exploiting this story to the local tourists, selling goods that visitors could buy to remind them of their visit.

Erica laughed at herself. She had enjoyed looking at the little tokens, despite the cheapness and fascination with material objects to reminisce about a visit to the island. A souvenir was an American tradition with children. Although fun and memorable, it was something she did not completely approve.

She believed that a child should not need a souvenir but be able to study and learn and then remember and tell instead of putting such value into a purchased good. She dismissed the fact that the islanders made money from the sale of these goods and that money helped the island economy.

She and Daniel had discussed an old legend many times and actually given it some scientific acknowledgement. She was a scientist, and mystery was not an option. However, the legends fascinated Daniel, and they overwhelmingly fascinated Vincent. This was the magic, and Erica respected the bond.

Unfortunately, Vincent was not around long enough to share this fascination with Daniel. He was always at work or, even worse, spending more and more time away, somewhere she did not want to consider. She had a life. She did not need confusion from a man who lived in her house. Between her career and duties as a mother, Erica let Vincent be. He was an artist by trade, an architect, and a dutiful companion to the work of sustainable society. He was absorbed in his work. He also brought vast amounts of money into their bank accounts.

Erica was a biologist doing research, and she used plenty of money from that bank account to fund her research. A team that was completely profit-free hired her, and it was funded mostly by grants, except her husband's contributions, which he urged Erica to use. He laughed about money and loved to make it. Erica, on the other hand, was a busy mother and working scientist. She had no time to think of money. So the family arrangement was an accepted way of life.

Erica thought about herself—educated, ambitious, and a little too controlling but nurturing. Daniel needed that kind of love. He thrived on it, but his quite capable father just seemed unable to give the extra affirmation Daniel needed.

Daniel called out, "Mom, it's getting dark. Let's get back to the house."

"All right," replied Erica, "but I must take one more recording. Why don't you go on without me?"

"I'll come back later." Daniel gathered his things and trudged to the car.

As Erica completed her data, she began to think of the many legends following this island lore. *Moonstone was a beach for those in love ... Walk the beach at night ... Travelers' delight ... Protection against perils at sea ... Calm the emotions ... and interestingly enough, ease hormonal and menstrual distress.*

Another old belief suggested that, while the moon was high and two people were wearing a moonstone, they would place the gemstone before their hearts, and then their love would be restored. Moonstone in the mouth would refresh memory. When the moon was waxing, the white spot in the stone actually became larger and dispelled negativity. It could also reconcile broken relationships.

This opalescent stone was meant to charm and heal. Erica thought of her love for Vincent and her devotion for her own child. Perhaps this was why they were bonded so closely but needed charm.

Daniel seemed content with life just the way it was. He had a rich life. He was a good student most of the time. And he had many friends, a few very close ones. He seemed happy tramping around Moonstone Island, always looking for adventures and stories.

Daniel and his pals would plan outings and spend hours exploring the nature-rich island with many species of birds and other glorious fauna. The surrounding beaches were lined with washed-up materials, more stones, and gnarled tree limbs delicately worn by the ocean's currents. And to their greatest delight was the wash-up of the new and ancient whalebones.

Daniel would also visit many people on the island, especially to listen to tales passed down from family to family. One of his frequent visitors was Old Man Drake Clark, who many believed was *loco*, a little odd in the head, because he told stories and legends linking the island to prophesy. Daniel took a great interest and enjoyed listening to the old legends that the old man revealed. Many mothers of the island doubted the old man. They did not approve of any visit to him, as they were leery of anyone who dressed like a bum and allowed his beard and hair to grow out of control.

Erica knew he was harmless. In fact, he did a world of good for Daniel. Daniel did not have grandparents, and the old man fit the role. So Daniel spent a great deal of time with the old fellow, listening to stories and helping him with errands. As the old man aged, his health began to fail. Even walking was a chore, so they helped each other with devotion.

CHAPTER 3

Marine Research

Erica's research team had commissioned her to take a two-week research study of the whale migration patterns and corresponding ocean temperatures. They were to travel far into the ocean and record the migration paths of the whales. This would be an arduous task, requiring long hours and steady sea legs. The water at this time of the year was cold and treacherous. Their team was chosen because they had proven quite valuable in the area of marine research.

Erica had concerns about being away so long. Daniel was capable of caring for himself, but she had never been away longer than three or four days. Vincent would have to spend extra time at home instead of working and vacating his patriarchal duties. Perhaps this was the perfect time for the two to reestablish a bond that needed to be grounded into something lasting and treasured.

When Erica announced that she was leaving, Vincent looked aggravated and perplexed. He did not like changes, especially the idea that he would need to be home in the evenings to help with dinner and chores and to help Daniel with homework.

"Erica, I don't know. I have several projects going on at the office, and they are all due to close in the next month. If I am away, they will not be completed on schedule."

Daniel piped in like a real trooper, "Mom, Dad doesn't

have to babysit me. Geez, I am almost fourteen. I can cook, clean, and walk Ernie."

Ernie was Daniel's Dalmatian, given to him when he was young. Unfortunately, the dog was a little unpredictable and would snap at people on occasion. But Daniel was able to keep him calm and in control. Erica wanted to be insistent and knew this was her call. Her husband would make a change, and if it weren't for her, at least it would be for her son.

She answered Vincent's remark, "I will expect you to be a father for a change." She left the dinner table, left the house, and took a long drive along the coast, not returning for several hours.

Daniel was shocked. He had never heard his mother speak so boldly, and needless to say, Vincent was livid. His quiet wife, tolerant and accepting, had never been so demanding. Vincent was aware that Daniel was uncomfortable and subtly beginning to understand the nature of his father's problem.

Daniel was not transparent and immediately began to clear the dishes off the table, leaving his dad in a quiet, sober mood. He went to the home office on the other side of the house to drown his scornful feelings.

Daniel was aware of his father's affliction, and he shrugged his shoulders. He didn't feel like finishing the dishes, so he grabbed a box of ice cream, ran to his room, and watched one of his favorite movies. He would fill his sour mood with something sweet and entertaining.

However, Daniel was not interested in the television. His mind was too alert and upset to watch the TV. So he grabbed a comforting book, one he had not read for a while, and began to leaf through the pages. This book had been his favorite almanac throughout his childhood. He and his peers would read the book at recess, and he would sometimes even insert the book into a language arts text if the teacher were droning on about parts of speech or some other teacher-derived vocabulary. His teachers had confiscated the book several times.

This Pokémon book was his kid bible, and it had been read many times. The frayed pages were a reminder of the devotion it spurred. This book was an escape into a foreign world in which anything could happen. His restless peers had also enjoyed reading and sharing the information. As Daniel scanned the charts and information, he noticed something new. How many moonstones were there? The chart said possibly four, including Pokémon Yellow, Special Pipachu.

Delighted and intrigued, Daniel decided to research the moonstones again. He went back to his gemstone journal and research folder.

Etymology
- Name derived from visual effect caused by light diffraction within the microstructures consisting of feldspar layers
- Also called hecatolite
- Two feldspar species, orthoclase and albite

Wow! thought Daniel. In 1970, *the moonstone was chosen to be Florida's state gem for the astronauts landing on the moon, even though the stone is not found naturally in the Florida. The Floridians must really believe in the legends and stories of the moonstone. Certainly, the Kennedy Space*

Center located in Cocoa Beach could contribute to the belief that the stone had some serious meaning.

Daniel continued his research online, going from one site to another as he had in his younger days with Pokémon manuals. Historically, moonstones were regarded in medieval legends and traditions. They were a good luck stone that supposedly gave the ability to foretell the future for close friends. Legends stated that it must be placed in the mouth while the moon was full.

If you buy your loved one a moonstone, you will love her forever. He turned this over in his mind.

As Daniel continued his search, he whispered to himself, "Moonstones are steeped in lore and legend. Cool. Just like Old Man Drake Clark. Weird though. I wonder why."

CHAPTER 4

Family Problems

Crash!

Something was happening in the house, thought Daniel.

He went to investigate. His mother had returned from her escape, and upon arriving, she had found Vincent sleeping in his office from a few too many tips of a bottle. She had thrown the bottle at the wall, and it had shattered.

Daniel ran back into his room. He was not ready to watch his mother cry and scream at his stupid, drunk dad.

CHAPTER 5

Daniel's Escape

Ah! thought Daniel.

And his escape continued with the moonstone legend research. Moonstones were associated with the Goddess Diana. The opalescent stone had a small, white spot that moved toward the center of the stone when the moon was full. It was known as a "wish stone" and was said to bring insight to the wearer. It was also used to dispel negative energy.

Rainbow feldspar, although pretty, might have infractions or inclusions, thus making it fragile. It was a popular stone during the 1930s. A Sri Lankan legend suggested that the Portuguese first found it in 1505.

The Romans called them *astrians,* meaning "star stones" or stairway to heaven. It was also related to the Sri Lankan Buddhists steps and 1906 Art Nouveau.

The moonstone pendant represented moonstone innocence. *The Moonstone* was a 1934 movie, a sinister, exotic mystery classic by Wilkie Collins. *The Moonstones* was also a novel published in 1868, written about an enormous yellow diamond.

According to an old Vedic myth, Lord Vishnu and the demon god Bali quarreled. Lord Vishnu prevailed, breaking Bali's body into pieces. As the body fell, it took the shape of gems and jewels. Thus, moonstones originated from the radiance of the pupils in Bali's eyes.

According to some old news and trivia of 1937, a

tiara made of moonstones and turquoise survived a terrible plane crash. It had been safely preserved in the strongbox. It was now on display at the Victoria and Albert Museum in London.

CHAPTER 6

A Mother's Love

Preparing for her scientific journey deep within the Pacific Ocean, Erica contemplated calling her sister Beth. She would make sure Daniel was attended to, but she truly wanted Vincent to show Daniel his best side. She did call Beth, who said she would call every day and check on Daniel.

Before she left, she and Vincent decided to have a quick lunch date at the local pub. Vincent did not like to take time off for something as trivial as a lunch date with his wife, but he complied at her insistence. They met in the old seaside tavern with tables and chairs made from the wood of old ships.

The pub was bright with many windows that revealed the beauty and serenity of the ocean coast. Here they were immediately reminded of their younger days, listening to the local rock music and enjoying the fresh fish of the day.

Again, Erica wanted to discuss her departure, and Vincent was astounded. She had never discussed the possibility of life without her. Vincent ordered another beverage and laughed it off. He was not serious about things that should never be ignored.

She looked him in the eye and demanded, "If anything were to happen to me, you must promise to change your ways. Spend quality time with Daniel. Let him know how much he is loved."

At this point, Vincent was angered out of his own guilt. Their marriage had really slipped down the rocks, and he was aware that it was his fault. He had some issues, and that bothered him. He also knew that Erica was aware and tolerant, but the look in her eyes told him to wise up. She needed the affirmation that he would always remain close to Daniel.

Vincent loved his son, and he had not intentionally distanced himself. He wanted to spend time with the kid—fishing, boating, and even helping him with his homework—but his work had become his life. Erica had been happy, or so he thought. She needed the earnings of his work to supply the resources of her research and study.

CHAPTER 7

Good Food, Happy Home

Early the next morning, Erica arose, brewed the roasted coffee, and heated the handmade cinnamon rolls. Erica loved to bake, an early morning pastime she had established during times of insomnia. But a night of tormented inability to sleep was not a pastime she had tolerated.

She scrambled eggs and added a few chives and tomatoes. Vincent was keen for the cinnamon rolls and all of her baked goods. Erica thought, *This is the one thing that seems to keep Vincent home and happy. Funny how such a complicated man could sometimes be so simple.*

Her boys were sleeping, and she loved the early morning, fiddling around the kitchen and thinking all was safe and sound. However, this morning was particularly special because she was departing for the project, for research that would satisfy a lifelong goal, it was not only a unique and exciting professional experience, it was a necessary departure that would possibly and hopefully reunite the lost bond between a son and father.

She would not worry about them. She had been a devoted wife and nurturing mother. They could get along well without her. Erica thought firmly to herself, *Why had I not done this before? I'm always so accommodating and tolerating.*

She quietly stepped into Daniel's room, which was decorated with stars and the constellations, a small saltwater aquarium, and miscellaneous collected shells, twigs, and stones. Erica realized these precious items were Daniel's souvenirs of his life. He had collected these things with her, his friends, and even his father.

She looked at the old leather ball glove that Vincent had given to Daniel. Even though they had never enjoyed the sport together, Daniel had treasured the mitt and wrapped it around a stuffed monkey that he'd had since he was a little tot.

She smiled, looking at her son, who was sleeping peacefully while wrapped in an old quilt made by her great-grandmother. *How happy he looked,* she thought. "Snug as a bug," her grandmother used to say to Erica and her brother.

She walked over to Daniel and gently awakened him. "Daniel, sorry to wake you. I must go now. Your breakfast is in the kitchen. There's fresh orange juice in the fridge."

Daniel looked up at her with his sparkling sprite eyes. "Thanks, Mom! Yum, I'm hungry." She gave him a little peck on the cheek, and he hugged her tightly and stated, "That's your bear hug, Mommy."

She hugged him back. "Don't you think of me as gone, for I am always with you, my darling child."

Daniel gave her a sappy look and said, "Mom, come on. I'm almost fourteen."

Erica smiled. "You are always my baby, and moms can get sappy with their children any time they want to."

Daniel plopped his sleepy head on the pillow and returned to dreamland. As Erica walked away, she heard him say quietly, "I love you, Mommy."

"All the way to the moon and back." With a tear in her eye, she closed the door and grabbed her jacket and hat.

The wind was blowing slightly. Erica began to think about her task. *Bad weather, not a good sign.* She had just about left the house when she thought of Vincent, who was passed out in their room, sleeping off his indulgence. *One small kiss for my other boy.*

She walked into the cozy room, walked over to her husband, and tapped him on the shoulder. "I am leaving now, Vincent."

Strangely, he grabbed her and plopped a big kiss on her mouth. *Wow,* thought Erica, *that was rare.*

Vincent was still mostly asleep but mumbled a little and told her to watch out for the riptides and stay to the north. *How odd,* she thought. *He had never been so elusive.* The kiss reminded her of a time when their love was new and fresh.

She hugged him with all her might and said, "I will see you soon, love."

He immediately sank back into a deep sleep. She left with a kick in her step. She had done a great thing, and her husband was already behaving like a husband again.

Erica shouted out one last demand, something she had never requested. With a loud voice, she stated, "Vincent, you behave!"

Driving to the pier, Erica was lost in thought. She had failed to notice the ominous clouds in the sky. Her mind was focused on the upcoming adventure. She was mentally preparing for the deep-sea research. Her gear was packed in the car, and she was ready to join the research team. The small ship was in the harbor, and the rest of the team had already arrived. They were loading the gear and speaking brightly about the voyage and work ahead. They had noticed the looming dark skies, but the weather report was good; the storm was supposed to pass, and they would be able to continue the work.

CHAPTER 8

Fearless Crew

Within the hour, the vessel was ready for the assignment. They were to spend the next two weeks recording ocean temperatures and attempting to monitor whale migration.

Erica and the team gathered in the ship's galley and discussed their course and plan for the departure. The boat moved quickly through the water at a steady speed of twenty knots. The morale on the boat was good, and all were inspired and ready to share their task. They knew how important their mission was.

CHAPTER 9

The Tempest

Erica and her dream team financed by miscellaneous and anonymous grants were moving steadfast and true. They seemed to fly over the churning waves with the wind at their backs and their minds moving forward. Their destination was not close, but the instruments were waiting. They had moved through the treacherous, storm-tossed ocean with diligence despite the hazardous conditions. Their writing journals were waiting to be filled with the data of the magic of the sea. Their minds were constantly taking in the information of the turbulence, the importance of their voyage.

The great sea was beginning to churn with great ferocity. The waves were high and kept landing their white-colored tips onto the moving vessel. Every warning was there, yet the team moved forward. They were determined and believed they could outrun the storm. They fought the tempest for many hours.

After two days, the team began to think of throwing an anchor or trying to find another way out of the storm. The helm was taking in too much water, and the constant roll of the boat was beginning to create problems in the electronic instruments.

The crew met in the galley to have a quick cup of coffee and discuss whether to return to the mainland or remain and fight the storm. They were only a day or so from their destination, so they decided to stay.

Within hours, the waves began to crash on the deck of the injured vessel. Most of the instruments were disconnected and covered for protection from the storm. The crew was on deck, chucking water or tying down ropes and cables. Erica had stayed below to put away instruments and secure the galley.

In one flash of lightening, a large wave hit, and the vessel fell to its side. The crew was at the mercy of the perilous storm. Erica grabbed a rubber raft that was not inflated. She realized that they shouldn't remain on the sinking vessel. She quickly inflated the raft and tried to move through the broken boat. She was able to exit, but the next wave, three times larger than the last one, took her to an unknown destination. She did not have time to know the treachery of the violent storm.

CHAPTER 10

Mainlanders Enduring the Wait

The islanders waited by the hour, tick tock and tick tock. The expedition was well known for its discoveries and commitment. The crew had been expected to return the day before, and with anxious apprehension, the villagers seemed to hold their breath. They were like a family in this small community. Daniel was worried, and Vincent took care of his fears with his frequent outings to the Hungry Traveler.

During the past twenty-four hours, waiting for his mother, Daniel feared the worst, but he found a way to be bright and hopeful, reminding his dad that the house was a semi-disaster and they needed to go the grocery store.

"Dad, Mom's going to freak when she sees this mess," Daniel said, trying to encourage his dad by reminding him of Erica's demands, but Vincent seemed lost in his own world.

Later in the day, Daniel walked to the edge of the sea and found himself sitting at the end of the pier, looking off into the horizon.

"Mom, I know you are there, and I know you are coming back." Daniel felt burning tears well up in his eyes, and he began to feel the pain of the loss of his mother.

He was not alone. Many of the islanders had been watching and waiting for the team. The community was solemn. They had watched the news of the storm at sea. The old fishermen were quite aware of the severe storms that occurred suddenly at sea. They waited apprehensively. The younger men, seamen of some sort either by labor or pleasure, ventured out, looking for signs of the returning vessel. But it was all to no avail.

"As is most storms at sea ... so shall they be ... returning to the mainland ... hand in hand," quoted Old Man Drake Clark, recognizing the cruelty of the tempest surrounding the crew.

CHAPTER 11

Completing the Legend

The approaching storm had the island people busily preparing for its aftermath. They had boarded up their windows and stashed food and beverages to wait out the storm. Some had even made plans to leave the island to stay with family or friends.

Daniel was not certain what he was to do. He was worried about his mother's welfare, and he did not think about himself. He did bring in his spotty old friend, who had been "barking up a storm." Daniel laughed at himself.

The Dalmatian quieted and sat nervously at Daniel's feet, looking into Daniel's eyes. Daniel knew at once that he must find his dad. His dad had been very peculiar for the past week. He had actually been around.

Well, sort of, Daniel thought. *At least he had stayed on the island at night, and he had been around twenty-four seven on the weekends. Wow. Dad is making an effort to follow Mom's instructions. A first for sure.*

But where had he been? Daniel knew: the Hungry Traveler, his parents' favorite date-night destination. *Well, it used to be,* he thought.

Daniel called his dad's cell, but his dad didn't pick up, so he left a voice message instead. He was probably despondent at this point.

"Ugh." Daniel sighed.

His dad's frequent visits to the pub usually ended with

a ride home from one of the local residents. But Daniel decided to venture out into the storm to fetch his dad.

"I'm going to get him this time," Daniel stated and quickly fed the nervous Dalmatian, who gobbled the dry food mix.

Daniel decided to pour a can of the wet stuff in the bowl. His dad often did this. Old Ernie was aging and losing weight, so Vincent, who had a very close tie with the dog, always gave him something extra. Daniel watched him lap up the canned dog food.

Daniel began thinking and felt some relief, just like the dog. After reading the label of the dog food can, he thought, *That canned dog food has more protein and nutritional value than most food for human consumption.*

He and his mother had used the theory as a science fair project. He thought it was gross, but he had cinched the contest and was given a cool microscope and several other gizmos. Daniel was stoked that his school actually gave prizes that initiated more learning, not just tree-wasting certificates.

Daniel sat down on the old wooden chair, a family heirloom that was over a hundred years old. His grandfather had given it to his mom when she went away to college. It was a cool chair, and Daniel enjoyed sitting there, especially now as he watched the old dog eat. He was concerned about his mom, but he knew she was with the team, they were fine, and all would be well.

Daniel was lost in thought. *Mom was always there—efficient, practical, smart, and yes, terribly practical. But Dad, on the other hand ... Wow, he always seemed to need direction.*

Daniel began to feel tired and leaned his head on the freshly painted white walls. Ernie had finished his grub, and he was cleaning his mouth with his soft paws. Daniel began to dream, and his mind was free to a time when Old Man Drake Clark had shared an old island legend with him and his mother.

It had been an afternoon of watching the weather. A storm was approaching rapidly, and Erica and Daniel had stopped by the old man's house. They had wanted to check in on him and drop off some fresh sweet corn.

The old man, with his chompers intact, enjoyed eating corn on the cob, especially dipped in warm butter and sprinkled lightly with salt.

The old man was quiet and contemplative that dark afternoon, so they urged him to talk. He seemed not completely coherent but nevertheless understood.

The old man began to speak, "You good folk know the old legend of the isle, eh?"

Erica smiled and sighed. "Yes, we do, Drake, and it didn't work for me."

"You gotcha a good son," remarked the old man boldly.

At that moment, she looked embarrassed and glanced at Daniel, who was not really thinking about the moonstone legend of love. Daniel realized then exactly what the old man had said.

Drake continued, "There is another old legend that none of ye youngsters are aware of."

"What might that be?" asked Daniel.

Drake continued and stated boldly, "This is the one that could save us all."

Erica looked away. She did not like some of the stories that the old man told, but she remained silent. Drake continued. He was a tea drinker and asked them to refill his mug with the steamy, boiling water from the old kettle.

Erica poured the water as the old man combed his mustache with his fingers. His eyes had a dreamy look, and the pupils seemed as blue as the sea on a bright day.

The old man rolled his words like an old poet, "The ancients say a big storm will pass this way, and it will engulf the island completely. Enormous waves will cover everything and everyone for miles around. It is an old island. Remember the bluffs on the northeast side, Daniel?"

Daniel nodded his head and immediately remembered the biggest bluff that towered into the air off the island. It was a very strange land formation, not quite understood but treasured by the old locals and visited by many tourists. People believed the moon dropped the stones there, and they would search for them. Most of the tourist shops made out like bandits because, of course, the ones to buy were easier and faster.

"That bluff," the old man exclaimed, "was a very old rock formation formed when the island was new. It was quite the tower of hope. The old villagers used to climb it and watch for ships, whales, or even approaching storms and waves." With a hard look in his deadpan blue eyes, the old man gazed into Daniel's eyes.

"The storm can be diverted, Daniel." He was serious and wanted Daniel to remember every word, and Daniel did.

Daniel, almost asleep on the old wooden chair, awakened with a start. Snapping back to reality, he listened to the wailing moans of the storm. Daniel realized he had been dreaming and knew that he must fulfill the legend.

Even the dog jumped up like a pup, ready to go, to help Daniel. Ernie was special and seemed to understand when Daniel needed help. Ernie also loved his old master, Vincent, who at this time was riding out the storm on a barstool with a couple of buddies, sulking their grief over a bottle of brew.

Daniel ran to the storm porch, grabbed his windbreaker raincoat, and pulled on his rubber boots. He looked at the dog and knew he would not be alone. As Daniel opened the door, the wind tore it out of his hands. It slammed into the outside wall, and there it remained, caught in the power of the storm.

Daniel and the dog began walking toward the Hungry Traveler with his head into the wind, feeling the cold rain beat on his young, tender skin. It hurt, but he pressed on. The storm would not stop him. Daniel was on his own mission, and nothing would stop him.

As he approached the tavern, the wind had seemed to ease. Daniel and the dog walked in. The place was almost empty except for his dad, the bartender, and a few others sitting at the tables, eating peanuts and drinking their dark brews.

Vincent looked up and retorted with slurred words, "Hello, Son, what brings you my way?"

Ernie tried to leap into Vincent's lap. Vincent sat back and patted the spotted coat of the old Dalmatian. Vincent arose from the old stool and saw the sense of urgency on his son's face. Slowly, the three left the inn, only after Vincent threw a fifty-dollar bill on the bar.

"Keep the change," he remarked.

The bartender smiled, and the group exited the tavern.

Daniel called out, "Wrap up tight and be ready for the blasting rain."

As they exited the warm tavern, entering a fierce and violent storm, Vincent was immediately sober. "Have you heard from your mom?"

"No, Dad. She is with the team.

Vincent started walking toward the shore, another direction.

"Dad, where are you going?" Daniel asked. Vincent kept walking, and of course, the old dog followed. Daniel shouted, "Dad, what is wrong? Why are you going toward the ocean?"

Vincent looked into his son's eyes, and immediately the son and his father knew they had met at a common truth. Daniel was surprised and full of relief when he realized his father was also committed to fulfill the legend, one Vincent had learned from his own pop, Old Man Drake Clark.

CHAPTER 12

Daniel and Vincent Become Heroes

Vincent was unstoppable, as if on his own mission. Daniel and the fearless family pet followed with urgency. Vincent was preoccupied and seemed determined to do something. As they walked closer to the ocean, the far side of the island, the figure of the tall butte came into site. Daniel could see its tall, thin, reaching peak, like a thumb pointing upward, despite the driving rain and heavy stormy gales blasting them with cold water.

Vincent called out, "Son, you know what you must do. I will take the dog down to the beach to locate the whalebones."

Daniel was shocked and thought, *My dad knows the legend, and never before had we ever done such an important task together.*

Vincent did know the legend, and little to Daniel's knowledge, he had learned it the same way, through a much-admired man, Vincent's father—his real father. Vincent had a very difficult time with these stories, all of them. Nevertheless, Vincent walked with a solid and sure stride.

Daniel watched him walk away with the dog in tow and thought, *He's going after the old whalebones resting on the deserted island shore.*

These bones were well preserved after years of floating in the ocean and drying in the sun. Not everyone—in fact, very few people—knew about this small, secluded beach. It was rumored to be haunted by the ghosts of the whales, past and present, which had died for unknown reasons.

Daniel, his mother, and his seemingly haunted dad knew but did not speak of it often. This was one of the reasons why Erica had become a marine biologist, specifically researching whale migration and ocean temperatures, looking for answers with hopes of finding a better way for people and for creatures of the sea.

Vincent, despite his problems, was also working side by side with Erica in his own way, distorted as it was. He financed Erica to work in the field, a penniless profession. Research was expensive, and equipment was beyond any scientist's financial earnings. This was why he was gone almost 24-7. His earnings from the architectural designs involving sustainability and earth-friendly shelter designs were highly guarded. He had to be away and completely confidential. His work was highly sought after. And for that reason, he remained away and preoccupied.

The absence of his family, for a greater need, was almost too much for this driven man. He substituted the love of his family for other desires. He knew Erica was the hero, and for that, he would sacrifice himself for the greater cause. Yes, what he did was not traditionally correct, but he realized that his purpose was more important, Erica, his soul mate, his wife, and the mother of his child, would prosper and fulfill the necessary duties to amend the past mistakes.

Daniel watched his father and waited, unsure but certain that what was going on was the correct thing.

Daniel thought, *What a dichotomy. I love my dad. He is my greatest hero.*

The truth was slowly becoming his dream. His joy was overwhelming. Tears filled his eyes. They were warm and healthy despite the freezing cold rain. Daniel's broken heart was rapidly repairing. For the first time, he and his dad were a team.

Daniel saw his father collecting the long whalebones. He had lifted two of the same size and weight. He then propped them on each of his shoulders and grasped the end of the bones in his hands. *Clever,* Daniel thought. *The only practical solution to carry the large bones, light but old and fragile.*

When Vincent returned to Daniel, the wind was blowing so loudly that they could not hear the words, but they knew the words because they knew the legend. Daniel had to carry out the remaining tasks. He was the chosen son, the person, the hero who could save the island.

Vincent approached Daniel and shouted, "Come with me, Daniel! We must climb the bluff."

Daniel realized that his father would climb the tower and deliver the bones, as he would collect the moonstones, the real ones left in a very discrete place, according to the legend. Together, the father-and-son team would fulfill the obligations, as Old Man Drake Clark told. As they began to ascend the bluff, the wind howled, and the rain fell and almost blinded their sight. The climb was rugged and exhausting. Vincent was out of breath, but he persevered. Nothing would stop him. Daniel sensed his father's courage and determination and followed him with zeal and enthusiasm.

After ten minutes of climbing, Daniel spotted the cave, the one with the five moonstones. Quickly, he entered the old, dusty, webbed cave with eyes darkened by the black night. He had to use his intuition and a handy small flashlight, to locate the moonstones. Daniel knew moonstones were always found near clusters of seashells and black rock.

The shiny rock, obsidian, was smooth but very sharp. Carefully, Daniel moved his hands over the mouth of the cave and followed the vein of the slate. And lo and behold, he finally located the five moonstones.

He put two in each pocket of his jacket and carried the fifth. This was the white one. He knew because he could see the center of light illuminating in the stone, now becoming brighter, glowing like a flashlight.

Vincent was amazed and then able to follow the small path that led him to the top of the bluff. As he approached, he looked out in the distance and saw the huge wave rolling in, ready to consume the entire island. Vincent caught Daniel's attention and encouraged him to proceed with care and caution.

Daniel waited for Vincent to set the bones in the correct position, like the joining of two letter Cs, forming a heart. Then the moonstones were arranged. All five were placed carefully to—according to legend—stop the impending storm.

Daniel placed the first stone at the tip of the joined bones with one on each side, horizontally and asymmetrically from the other. The fourth would be placed at the bottom on the formed heart. The last one, the glowing white one, was placed exactly in the middle, forming a streaming light glowing out into the dark, stormy night.

With their hands freed, they placed their palms on each side of the bone heart, and at that point, the air around them began to sparkle. As the flow of light extended into the black, starless night, the wind began to subdue, the howling stopped, and the thundering waves close to the island began to retreat.

Daniel and Vincent watched with awe. As the island began to feel the change, the vicious storm changed direction, and the sound of silence filled their world with peace again. With big eyes, they both looked to the ocean, and hovering in the sky was the shadows of the research team, the lost team, found in a blinding light that stopped the island from death and destruction. Somehow, the light between the moonstone and electrical instruments on the boat were joined and had created a charge that stopped the impending storm.

And on the deck, they could see Erica waving and smiling. She was a vision of beauty and light, and neither Daniel nor Vincent could move. They were enraptured with the vision, and together, they watched her slip away into another place. Their tears were cooled, and their hearts were joined together again. Like father, like son. United again.

CHAPTER 13

A Father's Love

No longer did Vincent stay in the old tavern, but he took more time to be with his young son, helping him with his projects. Vincent had decided to take a sabbatical. After losing his ladylove, he became sober and alert and at the helm of his family boat. Daniel mourned the loss of his mother daily, but his father and he had reclaimed the precious bond that linked their lives.

The storm and the treachery of another spooked the islanders. They did not know what had saved them. Only Old Man Drake Clark did.

The old man came out of his hiding and spent most of his time at the new museum. With anonymous donations, the city museum was built in honor of the lost scientific team. The museum also housed a library for research and instruction. Here, the legends were told, and scientific data about the whales and their migration, the moonstones, and many gemstones were gathered and shared for research and education.

CHAPTER 14

A Father's Love

Many years after the storm and the loss of Erica and her crew, a memorial was built in honor of the team, a floating statue. Actually, the base was anchored on the floor of the sea, and when the tides changed, the statue was either revealed or hidden, depending on the tides, thus appearing to be floating on the thundering surf.

At the top of the statue were the beautiful moonstone, the whalebone, and old legend unscripted into the statue. Very few actually knew it was there, but Daniel and Vincent were very aware and wanted to honor the legend and, of course, the team and Erica.

When the moon was full and the statue was revealed, a light was generated, sort of like a lighthouse. Many people began to visit the island and watch for the beautiful glow instead of tramping on the old weather butte, looking for the fake moonstones.

This time, the souvenir would live in their hearts, a glow for life, love, and learning.

Tonight, the moon is full, and the ocean is calm, but my heart beats to the sound of another heart, one so dear and true. This is the tale of my moonstone blues. From this day forward, I search for the blue moonstone shining tonight of all nights to remind us of true love and the beauty and sadness of the long-lost love.

A blue moonstone for a blue lady
A white moonstone for a white knight
Full moons are my heart's delight
Wish I may
Wish I might
Have his dream this one last night
Upon the island's edge
Near the sea bush hedge
Hearts together
True love is forever

About the Author

Cynthia S. Nolan is a 30-year veteran retired teacher with a Master's Degree. She is the author of Royally Courted, her first novel. She spends her free time hiking and enjoying long swims in the Pacific Ocean.

She and her daughter, Taylor live in Southern California with their Russian Ragdoll cat, Demetrius

www.ingramcontent.com/pod-product-compliance
Lightning Source LLC
LaVergne TN
LVHW020445080526
838202LV00055B/5339